Taking Kindness With Me

Jackie Chappell

ROURKE CLASSROOM RESOURCES

The path to student success

I take kindness with me when I stand in line and don't push.

I take kindness with me to the lunchroom when I sit with a new student.

I take kindness with me to recess when I follow the playground rules.

I take kindness with me when I visit my friend who is sick.

I take kindness with me when I say "thank-you" to the clerk at the store.

I take kindness home with me when I read a book to my little sister.

I take kindness with me wherever I go.